I0745213

GOLDFIELDS

A COLLECTION OF TREASURES BY LOCAL AUTHORS

First published by Accidental Publishing 2019

Copyright in this collection © Accidental Publishing 2019

The moral right of the authors has been asserted.

Cataloguing-in-Publication entry is available from the National Library of Australia
http://catalogue.nla.gov.au

ISBN 978-1-9259009-4-1 (paperback)
Fiction A808.3

Typeset in 10 pt Meridien Roman
Printed and bound by Ingram

Accidental Publishing
An imprint of Of The World Books
PO Box 8070 Bendigo South LPO VIC 3550
Australia
www.oftheworldbooks.com

Accidental Publishing

For all the readers and the writers who find
inspiration in Central Victoria

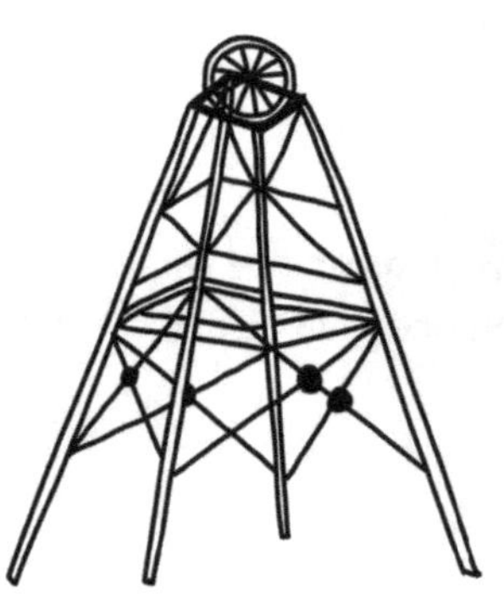

CONTENTS

8 **Foreword**
Rosemary Sorensen

13 **Agnes**
Sally Abbott

20 **Everything Is Colour**
Jess Anastasi

26 **French Sailor Gully**
Carmel Bird

32 **F Word**
John Charalambous

38 **This Cat's In Love With You**
Dianne Dempsey

46 **All That Glitters**
Amy Doak

52 **The Importance Of Knitted Squares**
Pam Harvey

59 **Dying For A Coffee**
Colin King

66 **Leap Of Faith**
Lauren Mitchell

72 **Profitable Envy**
Katrina Nannestad

79 **The Knowing Stone**
Steve Proposch

86 **Author Biographies**

FOREWORD

Down our road and around the corner, people have recently built a tiny house on what was once grazing land. It's on my drive into town, so for the past year or two, I've been checking out their progress. First, up went a very large shed, with solar panels on the roof. Then, in went a very large water tank alongside the shed. Months later, they started building the house.

Interesting, I thought. The big shed fronts the road. The tiny house is behind the shed. That's not the way it used to be done.

Then, in came all these bales of hay, long lines of them, striping the gently sloping land. Finally, staked seedling protectors – hundreds of them – cradled the tender stalks of little plants. Green plastic is ubiquitous in our neck of the woods, as newcomers like us and those neighbours down the road attempt to replant and restore land degraded by clearing and grazing.

I've loved watching the progress of these new neighbours. Simon and I have lived on our own bush block for nearly ten years now, and it still seems very new but also very much like our always-home. When we arrived, our land had been planted up by the people who built the house we now live in, and they had chosen an all-native garden, which nevertheless they must have had to nurture with hard work through drought years. The year we came, it bucketed down, the dam filled up, everything sprouted and the birds proliferated. Each summer now, most bushes and trees survive. Come autumn, if the rains come, you can hear the plants breathing out, exuding green smells and blossoming with tiny flowers.

That first year, I learnt a bit about water, and the way it moves across land. I don't think I've ever been as happy as I was then, sloshing through puddles with a shovel to channel water away from the flooded bits. Pete next door – who is never as happy as when he's behind the wheel of his ancient tractor – chuckled at the muddy sight of me, with a broad grin on my face. "Mucking around with water", we agreed, is our idea of a good time

But I had so much to learn – and I'm not saying that with a downward inflection, denoting disapproval of that younger self. Hear my voice rising upwards in tone and with a smiling lilt: I had so much to learn!

For instance – the obsession with dams and bores, even on farming properties but certainly on tree-change properties like ours, is odd. *Pace* Pete-nextdoor, but bulldozing a great big hole is rather silly, given that in summer it all evaporates anyway, and given that a long, snaking channel is going to work much better for water retention.

From the neighbour the other side, I learned to love bushes that don't fit the conventional idea of beauty. Early on, he tried to point out to me that poisoning Sweet Bursaria was not a good idea. This spiny plant, which is the only host for the endangered Eltham Copper butterfly, was popping up everywhere across a patch of our place, and I stupidly thought that was bad. Sweet Bursaria – like the honey-fragrant needlewood which the black cockatoos adore, like the ever-flowering Westringia that the honeyeaters fossick in all year round – is a very special plant, gloriously messy, subtle in its blossoming, a haven for small birds. When a new one pops up now, I punch the air.

Again, I look back on that former me with a sort of wonder – not that I was stupid, even though I was, but that I have had the opportunity to learn, to know better. A kind of enlightenment.

I don't want to be angry at the harm done by people who came to this part of the world in quest of riches, displacing with violence the people who lived here, cruelling a delicate landscape, poisoning what they couldn't perceive as useful or beautiful. I want instead to think about people like the new neighbours, as I watch their optimistic toil, and the way they are transforming the bit of land they are husbanding.

I'm grateful to this Bendigo, this Central Victoria, for that opportunity to learn about such optimism, hope and joy, about the deep and real pleasure of feeling at home in a place. And in the same way, I'm grateful to Amy Doak, with her excellent publishing capabilities and her energetic optimism, for creating this book of stories by and about my home place. I'd like to think that it's all connected: I watch those neighbours, I read these stories, I am part of it, it is part of me.

We are all custodians: of land, of stories, of life itself. These brilliant short stories, written by people with talent and expertise, are like the staked green plant protectors helping us all to grow. May they proliferate wildly across our entire region.

– Rosemary Sorensen
(Director, Bendigo Writers Festival)

AGNES
by Sally Abbott

The old garden shapeshifts in the pale dawn mist, looming and retreating, and looming and hiding again, whispering to itself or to the moon halo or to the shadows that shuffle forward and back and round-about, hungry black cat and witch's hat lonely shadows, sighs and mutterings about the breaking down world. It seems fragile, this garden, and haunted and sad: the small fruit trees, the quince and the lemon and the cumquat, bowing low under the weight of the cold grey and damp, yellow leaves falling, the silver gum ghostly, the garden beds beside the cracked front path dark and ragged.

Agnes Coventry shrugs the collar of her dressing

gown closer over the back of her neck and shoulders, and pulls the frayed green rug tighter over her knees. Her shoulders are sore, she notes, and her feet. And her hands. She is watching her garden sigh and shift in the gloom, icy teardrops of frost falling silently, slowly, one by one by one, from the gutter running against the long line of the front veranda, small cold pools forming on the veranda floorboards, water seeping down to the dust and dirt and debris beneath the house, the rusty nails and wood shavings and empty tin of paint and soft drink cans left behind long ago by laughing workmen and the thin, hard bones of a rat that died after eating the bait Agnes had put down the winter before last, or the winter before that perhaps, and beneath the rat bones and the cans, the harder dirt and rocks and the older decay and the lost and forgotten stories. Agnes is only imagining the frost water dripping and pooling and seeping, the chill of it, and the smell of cold, and the traces of the long ago workmen, and the brittle white rat bones. She imagines that is what is there, in the grey mist, and on and under her front porch. After all, most of a life is an imagining. Agnes knows this. Imagining is a hoping. A hanging on.

On many early mornings over the forty-seven years she has lived in the house, Agnes has sat in a chair by her bedroom window and watched the dawn uncurl and stretch. In the first years it was a heavy and ugly wooden chair from the heavy and ugly dining table her former husband had chosen and then insisted she have along with the two three-seater green leather sofas with fold away footrests and the faux marble coffee table when he finally understood and accepted the marriage was over and he walked away.

When she could afford it, Agnes arranged for the dining table and chairs and the sofas and coffee table to be taken to a charity. She attached a note to the table – I am sorry this is all so ugly, but hopefully someone might like it. My ex did. And then she bought a big white wicker chair with white cushions that sat handsomely against newly painted white walls and soft white curtains. By the time the wicker chair began coming undone, Agnes was tired of white, tired of trying to keep things, everything, light and bright and just so. She wanted colour again. Warmth. Wood. Textures. Surprises. Mess. She undid her white house, stripping back window frames and doors to their original hundred hues, taking up the carpets, painting bookshelves green and blue and cream. She found lampshades and cushions and pots in big, laughing colours. For a time the little house was made bolder and brighter and

Agnes always thought, when she could bear to, that those were her happiest years. Unpredictable. Strange. New worlds and ways, or old. But happy. I had that much, she often reminded herself. It was something.

Now Agnes sits in a vast red armchair, faded in patches, worn thin on the arms, dog and cat hair caught in the creases. From here she watches the mornings descend, the faint spring mornings, still, despite it all, suggesting hope in their softness and bursts of birdsong, the fierce and shocking white summer mornings, the shuffling grey winter dawns. She watches also the street beyond her front gate, the street that feels to her like a living being, a thing grown old and odd and overburdened and tired, creaking and breaking. Just like me, she thinks. Why do we never really stop to think that it comes to this? Addie said: we take a lot of care to not know things. It's the only way through. Good morning Addie. Good morning to you.

The autumn dawn has fully arrived now and Agnes contemplates the day. It is time to walk down the hallway to the kitchen and put the kettle on for a cup of tea. Two and a half minutes and fifty-three shuffling small steps. A bowl of cereal, although she is not hungry in the slightest. Food for the cat. She must put the television on and try not to hear what today's horrors are. If the television is not turned on, there might be a knock at the door later in the day and a brisk young person, down from Bendigo Surveillance Centre in the blink of an eye, computer in hand, standing there to size her up and down and assess her fitness for continuing to live as she lives. It may not happen, but it could. The stories are all about. And after all Julie was taken last year. They still talked about it at the monthly Bad Things Club meeting. So, television on. Say to the system, I am functioning. I continue to be. She will check to see if the Green Child has been. Eighteen shuffles to the back door and deck. Agnes had left a food parcel and a blanket on the outdoor table yesterday afternoon and she hopes they are gone. She will see. Then time to dress. No shower today. One more day won't hurt. The doctor's appointment is not until 10.30, so there is plenty of time. There is always plenty of time now. Agnes will get there early because it will be warm in the offices and she can sit and watch the queues and the people and the children and the tired doctors coming and going and listen to what they are saying to each other. She is grateful to have an appointment although she knows it is only because she is really quite unwell. Very unwell. And that is the conversation that must be had. Agnes has made notes on what she wants and needs to say, and she has rehearsed the conversation with the cat several times. And afterwards, when it is over, she will pick up whatever medications might be prescribed and buy a salad sandwich for her dinner from the fancy deli in the shopping centre. An expensive treat, but if she has to eat something later she wants it to be a salad sandwich. With a glass of wine.

And with the sequence of the day sorted, it is time to move. To get out of the chair. Here I go, Agnes says to the window. Here I go. The cat meows loudly in the kitchen.

You go girl, Addie says. You've got this.

I do. I think I do.

Then, while Agnes eats her cereal and yoghurt, Addie says loudly: Dignity. Irreducible human dignity. You remember that. It's all that there is, in the end. Well, not all, but you know what I mean.

The cat has put her paw in the cereal bowl and has shaken milk and yoghurt and oat flakes onto the table. I know what you mean, Addie. I always did.

On the television, there are images of an overcrowded cargo boat carrying female refugees from America trapped in an island of rubbish outside the entrance to Sydney harbour. The huge boat and the plastic island are pitching in rough seas and women are on the deck waving and screaming at the helicopters that are flying overhead to film them. The story is about how the boat can be freed from its plastic island and then where it should go and whether fresh drinking water can be delivered to it because there is no water left on board and already some women are dead or dying.

Human dignity indeed.

Don't watch, Addie says.

NOTE:
'Agnes' is an extract from Sally's current work-in-progress.

EVERYTHING IS COLOUR
by Jess Anastasi

I never knew when the drive through the centre of town was going to result in The Question. The question I always answered without really thinking about it.

"Mum, can we stop at Rosalind Park and go on the playground?"

The answer was mostly the same with only slight variations on the theme. "Not today, sweetheart. We're going to be late for dancing."

It might have been a few days or a week before I heard it again. "Mum, can we stop at Rosalind Park to see the big teddy statue?"

"Not today, honey. It's pouring rain. We'll come back when the weather is better."

But the day of better weather hadn't come next time I got asked The Question. "Mum, can we stop at Rosalind Park and climb the tower?"

"Not today, darling. We've got groceries in the car that I need to put away in the fridge at home."

Anyone who has kids knows they're persistent little ratbags when they want to be.

"Mum, can we stop at Rosalind Park and see the bats?"

This time a sigh accompanied the words. "Not today, my lovely. You've got homework to do and I need to get dinner started. Besides, bats sleep during the day, so there's not much to see."

That answer led to a lengthy discussion about where the bats had come from and why they hang upside down and why they can't see very well, littered with questions I only knew half answers to and a promised trip to the library to find a book about bats.

But the trip to the library went much the same way as my future promised stops at Rosalind Park.

The Question was stuck in her mind like a broken record, however. Ambushed on me when I least expected it.

"Mum, can we go to Rosalind Park today please? Remember at the Easter Fair when we searched for the creatures in the fernery? I want to do that again."

"The creatures won't be in the fernery today, that was just special for Easter. And we can't stop today, we've got an appointment to get to."

Sometimes, The Question was prompted by outside influences and I sternly reminded myself that surely I could have driven through town without going past Rosalind Park.

"Mum! There's something on at the Conservatory! Can we stop and see what it is? One time I went with Aunty Lisa and we got to dig up dinosaur bones."

"It might not be something for kids, and I've got work to get finished. I'm sure there'll be something there in the school holidays and maybe Aunty Lisa can take you again."

This time I got a huff for my troubles, but not much in the way of an argument. But she always asked when we were busy or in a hurry to get somewhere. And when I had time to spend with her, neither of us remembered.

I didn't notice when The Question stopped being asked. Suddenly we could drive past Rosalind Park and I wouldn't hear a peep. But I never noticed. I was too busy thinking about work and bills and appointments and school commitments and the million other little details that overflowed our lives in an unending torrent.

"Mum," she said thoughtfully one day while

we were waiting at the fountain for the complex changing of green and red lights around the intersection. "You know what I really love?"

"What's that, chipmunk?" I asked distractedly because most of my thoughts were occupied with trying to work out what to make for dinner, what was in the fridge or cupboard, what wouldn't take much time or effort to throw together, what would cause the least amount of complaints from three kids who all like completely different things.

"I really love this time of year when all the leaves change colour and fall from the trees. Some are just brown, but some are yellow, orange and red. And in some places, like in Rosalind Park, so many leaves fall on the ground it covers the grass in big piles. It's so much fun to run through them."

Silence followed the wistful words and the traffic started moving forward. Whatever I was thinking about before had completely left my mind. All I could see in my head was memories rising from a place I didn't even know existed inside me. Walking through Rosalind Park back when there were more dirt pathways than paved footpaths and the grass was patchy. Kicking up the leaves and laughing. The autumn sunshine warm on my face, but the breeze chilly on my arms.

Other long forgotten memories surfaced.

Venturing in after dark to see the possums racing up and down trees and edging curiously near feet, looking for food. Sunny afternoons spent sitting on the top of the tower with friends instead of in class, looking at the town spread out around us and wondering what the future would bring. Romantic walks on mild evenings sharing ice cream and talking about things I don't recall any longer. Rainy days jumping puddles and listening to the hushed patter of raindrops hitting the tree leaves far above.

I pulled the car into the first parking space I could find, and she looked at me with wide eyes, confused with a hint of excitement.

"Mum, what are we doing?"

"You want to run through the leaves, don't you?"

The confusion deepened, and a hint of suspicion joined it. "But don't we have to get home or something?"

"Not today. Today we're going to Rosalind Park."

She didn't need me to say anything else — out of the car in a second flat. When I joined her on the footpath, it was like seeing things for the first time in years. Like I'd been looking but not really noticing. Everything was colour. The green grass, the blue sky, the changing leaves. And she ran into that colour, reminding me of what it'd felt like to be young and carefree and exhilarated by something as simple as running through the fallen leaves.

That was the day we always started stopping at Rosalind Park. The day she didn't even ask The Question. And she never had to ask it again.

FRENCH SAILOR GULLY
by Carmel Bird

Extract from the journal of Heinrich Muller, September 25, 1913. Railway Hotel, Castlemaine, Victoria:

You may wonder why I am writing in my journal so far from my home in Vienna. This small rural Australian town is where I came in my latest search for my brother Franz who disappeared from the face of the earth in 1852.

I have waited many years, perhaps a lifetime, to resolve this riddle. So here I am, at the age of sixty-one, talking to Larry Chan, a Chinese man who long ago sold picks and spades and tin dishes to the miners at a place called the Forest Creek. He took me out to French Sailor Gully which was, he said, the place where a French miner drowned when the waters of the Forest Creek invaded and inundated the claim where the French sailor was working. It happened very swiftly, and the Frenchman could not be saved. "Franz, his name was Franz. Nobody could understand him, and he was a sailor, so we just called him French Sailor. He was very young, and we never knew anything about him. After he drowned we called the place French Sailor Gully. He had a big grey cat that ran away after his master died. We buried him here. Other men took his boots and his tools. He did not have any gold."

The low bushes and rough spindly trees had covered all trace, as far as I could tell, of the events at French Sailor Gully, sixty-two years before. Nothing remains but the silence, and an eerie stillness. Was this the burial place of my brother Franz who disappeared a year before I was even born? I believe it was.

Franz was only seventeen when he left our home in Vienna one night in the spring. He was suffering from a broken heart, and was never seen again. All my life he was mourned for dead. He had been madly in love with Louisa, the daughter of my father's darkest enemy. Perhaps it was like the story of Romeo and Juliet, in some ways. A week before Franz disappeared, Louisa's family whisked her away to a convent somewhere in Germany.

I have heard the story, the legend, of the night before Franz disappeared so frequently that it is almost as if I had been there at the time. He was a powerful presence in the family, in the house, in my heart. All my life my mind has quietly hummed with little summaries: "He ran away to sea. He ran off to find Louisa. He took one of the horses. He joined the army. He went to Paris. My cousin saw him on the beach in Rio de Janeiro. He fell in love with a dancer in Berlin. He entered a monastery, a remote monastery, in Belgium. He ran away to sea, and ended up, as sailors often do, seeking his fortune on the goldfields of California. Or perhaps even on the goldfields of Australia. Far, far away. He ran away to sea."

So, the night before Franz disappeared, my mother, who was given to prophetic dreams and visions, had a presentiment of disaster. As she was slumbering beside my father in their high, deep featherbed, she awoke with a start. Was she dreaming, or did she really hear the ring of a horse's hooves on the cobbles of the courtyard below? She lay still for a long moment – in years to come she always said she could not forgive herself for this time lost – until she folded back the silky coverlet and crept to the window where she parted the curtains and peered out. Moonlight fell on the cobblestones of the empty courtyard. The heavens were striped with soft grey cloud. A faint breeze disturbed the line of poplars bordering the approach to the house. No horse, no human presence. A large grey cat, still as a statue, was sitting on the edge of the stone fountain as if contemplating some distant reality. Slowly the animal turned its head towards my mother. And what my mother saw, plainly in the moonlight, was that the face of the cat was the face of my brother Franz. He was smiling sadly. They seemed to stare at each other for a long long time, spellbound, my mother said. And then before her very eyes the cat just disappeared. Faded. Dissolved. One minute it was there and the next minute it was gone, and the moonlight fell upon the cobbles and upon the fountain, and upon the empty, empty courtyard. The cat was never seen again.

She hesitated to awake my father, but she lit a candle, and in her long white nightgown she tiptoed urgently along to the room where Franz would be sleeping. There, beside the bed, a candle was burning low. The bed had not been disturbed. And Franz was never seen again. My mother knew in her heart that something strange and even terrible had happened. She ran back to my father and they, together with our old servant Peter and also my three sisters, searched high and low. Nothing.

In the days that followed, in the weeks, the years that followed, they conducted an exhaustive search for my brother. I was born a year to the day after that dreadful night.

As for Louisa, she returned to Vienna after many years, residing in the Convent of Saint Elisabeth, until she died in 1912. And then it was that a nun at the convent asked me to call on her, for she had something of some significance to tell me. And so I came to learn at least a part of the story of my brother's disappearance. For in the papers left by Louisa was a letter from Franz, sent from the distant goldfields of Australia in 1853. He gives the simplest details of his adventures, being intent upon assuring Louisa of his undying love. He will make his fortune, and will return in triumph to claim her as his bride. He explains how he took ship first of all to England from where he set out for New South Wales, working as a deck-hand. The letter is full of youthful confidence and optimism. Finally, he made his way to the diggings at the Forest Creek, some seventy miles or so from the golden city of Melbourne. He was known by the other miners as 'French Sailor', for nobody understood him when he spoke.

Larry Chan and I stood in the forlorn and haunted

gravesite at French Sailor Gully, and I said a quiet prayer. From the earth I gathered up a handful of crumbling orange dust, mingled with the fragments of dead sticks and leaves. I dropped the little collection into the pocket of my coat.

"We never did know who French Sailor was."

"I believe he was my brother."

F WORD
by John Charalambous

A scrawny old cat crashes Jojo's ceremony. I notice him meandering between the legs of the canvas chairs, then out in the open. He belongs to the people who bought our bush block eleven years ago. Very generous, agreeable people. Or maybe Mum just bulldozed them. Who can say no when she puts the pressure on?

The cat moves stiffly. He has a bad eye and baldy ears, a kink in his tail. He's at death's door. Yet he has dragged himself all the way up the ironstone hill to the Swing Tree. He fills the space between the front row of chairs and the lady saying nice things about Jojo. He looks at my brother and me, a hint of outrage in his green eyes.

I expect he will get to know my sister in days to come, after we've gone. He will sniff at her grey ashes under the tree. I can see why Mum chose this place. Here in Bendigo we were a family for a while, a man and a woman and three kids. We had a Biblical shape. The tree says it all. It has an age-old look, huge and twisty with low branches you can sit on. I can remember her nursing Jojo on the 'swing' while my brother and I played with our toys in the dirt.

The lady saying nice things about Jojo seems always to have existed in our lives. Mum collects such people – helpers, allies, women with oversized hearts. I think her name is June. She is or was a civil celebrant. Age has drained off some of her authority and charisma. I find her slightly dotty in her purple woollen poncho and feathered earrings. But Mum is beaming through her tears, my brother holding her hand, as June recites a series of haikus by a famous Japanese poet. One runs: 'This dewdrop world is but a dewdrop world, and yet –'

I guess the cat is part of the dewdrop world. I'm looking into his skewed eyes. I'm thinking about Jojo's F-word.

At four my sister started to 'speak'. 'Fun' or 'fan' she seemed to say, or sometimes 'foo-foo,' mashing the sound with her usual wetness, all breath and bubbles. It was Mum who decided this was more than random noise. She was up against the doctors, who all declared that her daughter would never develop the capacity for abstract thought. They found sensitive ways to say that she would remain forever a child of sensation, absorbed in the closed-off dramas of her body.

"Have you ever heard such crap?" Mum railed.

Dad was empty and demoralised. He knew the doctors were right. He also knew that Mum had become a sort of bomb loaded with love and despair and pigheaded violence. He said things like, "Who knows what's going on in that little head?"

It wasn't such a little head any more. Jojo was a big girl. Beefy. And less manageable now that she was growing long-bodied and strong. Sometimes, in a cranky mood, she toppled her special chair. I thought it would be easier to plonk her on the sofa rather than continue the pretence that she could join us in family conversation. We could all do without the hassle, not least Jojo herself, who certainly didn't need the excuse of a fall or a bump on the head to launch into a fury. At least once a week she screamed the house down.

There was only one way to calm her. Dad's way. We called it 'patting the cat'. He'd spent a lot of time petting animals as a boy, mostly his cat.

Both my brother and I became experts. You laid Jojo across your knees and massaged her spine. This was how you talked to her – with your fingertips. You kneaded the soft chicken-flesh around her vertebrae, you finger-walked over the bones, you traced the delicate whorls at the nape of her neck, and soon she was crying less wildly, and eventually going quiet between sobs, hanging limp like a dead thing and dribbling down your leg.

This didn't satisfy Mum. She longed for real human communication. "See, there she goes – fan fan fan."

"Yep, she's saying it," my brother and I agreed. We were fed up with the great Jojo circus, but understood Mum's need.

Dad ate breakfast with us after night shift. It was family time. He was being his best self, though it didn't always work. Jojo huffed and moaned. She clacked her teeth on the spoon. Mum reported developments: how my sister had said 'fan' on cue for Tina, the support-worker who came two days a week. Tina was just a girl with a dodgy certificate, a kid not long out of school, but still an independent witness. I remember Mum laughing, poking Jojo playfully in the tummy.

"Sometimes it's fan and sometimes it's fump. I wish she'd make her mind up."

"She's in a fump mood," Dad joked. "Everyone has fump days."

Mum said, "Maybe I'm her fump. To hell with plain English. She's going for a whole new language. I'm her fump and you're her fumpo." She laughed, but her idea, her revelation, had no solidity.

June the celebrant is off on a Buddhist flight. She waves a gnarled hand, indicating the tree, the brown autumn bush, maybe the universe. She's invoking the infinity of time. My sister is continuing her journey through the infinity of time. She is refining the beauty of her consciousness. I don't know whether Mum believes his stuff. The tears run down her face. Maybe my brother is crying too. He won't show himself. I feel the urge to fill my hands. It seems the most natural thing to make a lunge for the cat. He springs away, surprisingly agile for an old skeleton.

Mr Fromme killed the F-word. He was the specialist that saw Jojo every two months. He witnessed my sister's new trick, but was not as impressed as Mum thought he should be. He denied her hope that it might be the first sign of language. Jojo was simply discovering new aspects of her body and what it could do. She took pleasure in bubbling her lips. She took pleasure in wiggling her fingers. Now she took pleasure in a nice noise that she could make at will.

This was no small thing. She was growing her world. But it didn't mean she could, or ever would, employ sound to refer to things in an instrumental way.

Mum returned home saying Mr Fromme was an idiot. She dropped him and found another specialist. Jojo hit on new sounds. I can't deny she had a repertoire. But these new words never held the promise of the F-word. The nervous shimmer left my mother's eyes. And a couple of months later Dad had disappeared too. They sold the land.

The cat jumps, startled by the movement of feet. For June has called us up by name. We are to give Jojo back to the universe. Mum hugs me and my brother pops the circular cap of the container. We take turns emptying it out, flurrying human dust at our feet. Mum's friends are very still, as if not daring to breathe, while the cat scowls at us from beyond the tree.

THIS CAT'S IN LOVE WITH YOU
by Dianne Dempsey

Let me be clear about this – a phrase much overused by politicians – but let me be clear. Spit was no rogue cat, no desperate, wild thing you might find snarling at you from your back fence, beset by fleas and bald patches. It is true, Spit did not have a pedigree or a post-graduate degree for that matter, but Spit did have class.

Spit was the most magnificent cat to live in Belgravia, which was the name once given to a rather grand old part of Bendigo that surrounds the Sacred Heart Cathedral. Inspired by London's Belgravia, the Bendigo goldmine owners, the wealthy merchants and bankers built their mansions in the Italianate, pseudo Gothic style and gloried in their opulence. Today, those houses are still there.

Spit was purchased from a pet shop when he was about six-months-old by the Montrose family which at that stage consisted of Mrs Mary Montrose and Max and Mia, her grandchildren. The family had a mild but persistent addiction to alliteration. The 150-year-old brass name plate by Mrs Montrose's front door simply bore the name 'Montrose'. No need to say more.

Mrs Montrose took her grandchildren shopping one winter morning with the express purpose of acquiring a significant distraction. Her son and his wife had recently taken themselves off on a grand tour – a 94-day world cruise which featured a tranquillity bed with 1,000-thread-count linens.

"Why not, why not round off the trip to one hundred days, throw in the Seine cruise," Mrs Montrose had responded when her son and daughter-in-law had requested she care for the children in their absence. It was a sarcastic retort which she was to immediately regret as they took up her offer with gusto.

While walking down Rowan Street, on the way to the pet shop, Mrs Montrose saw her recently acquired neighbour Kristy Turner. Married to Dr Turner (Ear, Nose and Throat, ENT) and the mother of Olivia (plaits and a new oversize Girton Grammar uniform). Kristy had just finished supervising the attachment of her very own name plate which she felt had a vaguely ancestral tone. The Montrose family crossed the road to inspect "Highgrove".

"Very nice Kristy," Mrs Montrose told her. "But you know the house's original name?"

Kristy looked at Mrs Montrose suspiciously. "What?"

"The Paddock – the previous owners, the-Howards-lovely-people, made a squillion from their wheat and sheep property aeons ago."

"The Paddock? I haven't heard of a house named that before?" Kristy practically squealed.

It was then that Max and Mia saw young Olivia pick up a stunning Siamese cat which was cautiously walking towards them.

"Do you mind if Mia has a pat?" Max asked.

Although his sister was older than him, Max understood her shyness. But Olivia grabbed the cat and squashed it to her chest.

"You can't touch Cleopatra, she's going to be in cat shows."

"Don't worry about it," Max said. "We're going to buy our own cat."

Somewhat embarrassed by her daughter's rudeness, Kristy swiftly pulled out her phone from the back of her Dolce and Gabbana jeans. "Perhaps the children would like to catch up for a play date some time? Thursday week between five and six?"

"We'll check our diaries later in the day," Mrs Montrose said, "Goodbye Kristy." As they continued their walk Mrs Montrose muttered, "Arrivistes."

Max shook his head in disgust, "Cleopatra."

Pushing their fingers through the wire mesh of the pet shop cage, the children tried in vain to touch the six kittens dozing in an anonymous ball of fluff. But one kitten, the largest of them all, detached himself from the rabble and started to preen and purr.

He had a marvellous white chest and ginger coat and for the benefit of the children, he embarked on a sequence of pirouettes and arabesques and finished with a grand jete. Finally, he approached the children and touched their fingers with his paw.

Why was this big kitten still there? And why was he so enamoured of the children? Mrs Montrose wondered. And then the light dawned. Mia, her darling 12-year-old granddaughter had red hair. Ten-year-old Max had less distinguishable, brown hair but in Mia, the cat saw his own likeness, and he liked it. He longed to be in her arms where their ginger hair could mingle in one glorious, soft coat. It was not a matter of the children choosing the kitten but the kitten choosing them.

The kitten may have had an affinity for Mia but

when the shop owner tried to place it in a pet box, it spat, snarled and scratched him. The shop owner, who spent his weekends riding with a biker gang, took Mrs Montrose aside and suggested she have the cat knackered as soon as possible. "Imagine what he'll be like when those balls drop. And his name's Spit. Just seemed natural."

Of an evening at Montrose they played 'Cruises', just like Mum and Dad. Spit and Mia would curl up in front of the fire and Mrs Montrose would take orders – hamburgers, chips, ice cream, chocolates – it was bliss all around.

The children's parents had made arrangements for Max and Mia to attend Girton Grammar, which was just a few houses away from Montrose. Max made friends easily but Mia sat alone. Olivia had been asked to keep Mia company but Spit, watching from the vantage point of a peppercorn tree, observed that Mia was quite neglected. There was however another little girl, about Mia's age who also sat alone.

Spit made his way back to the Turners where he waited for Cleopatra to slip outside and smell the grass. Spit had been watching the Turner's home for several days and decided the only thing between him and complete happiness was the death of Cleopatra, who was definitely living on his territory.

Spit didn't have to wait long. Cleopatra was

languorously walking down her garden path when Spit took off and ran across the road. Unfortunately a car sent Spit flying through the air but he landed on all fours, shook his head and continued the chase. Cleopatra ran inside her cat door. Undeterred Spit bashed on through and cornered Cleopatra in the laundry. Cleopatra jumped onto a ledge where Kristy had the bathroom curtains soaking in a bucket of red dye. Spit leapt after Cleopatra, knocked over the bucket and continued the chase into the hallway where the boards had just been re-polished and were still wet. The sticky surface slowed both cats down as their now red little paws stuck to the surface. Kristy, who was by now hysterical, picked up a bust of Beethoven and threw it at Spit. It did stun him for a moment, giving Kristy enough time to lock Cleopatra in Olivia's bedroom and chase Spit out of the house.

Kristy crossed the road to speak to Mrs Montrose. Firmly. Spit hid with Mia in her room where the two of them listened: Spit must be put down, roasted on a barbecue, shot at dawn. Mrs Montrose told Kristy there was more than one ginger cat in the neighbourhood. In fact she was sure the presbytery housekeeper had recently acquired one. Mrs Montrose could be a spectacularly imaginative liar when cornered. Later she comforted Mia who thought she was in danger of losing the only friend she had in this god-forsaken town where the rattle of trams and the pealing of church bells haunted her dreams.

As usual, the first thing upon awakening, Spit wrote his list of jobs to do. First job, the playground. He met Mia and Max at lunch time where he allowed a group of children to cuddle him. The business of culling wasn't too difficult. He scratched and bit at the adoring children until finally there was one girl who remained. She was the new girl. She was a loner and she was tough, but Spit sensed she was kind. Spit left Mia talking to the tough but kind girl about their newly acquired, favourite subject, Spit.

Second job. Spit waited until Kristy went out shopping and Cleopatra was home, alone. Entry was too easy, the cat door. But wait, Dr Turner had nailed it shut. A quick reconnoiter however revealed a slightly open bedroom window. Spit softly padded through the house and found Cleopatra on the couch watching *High Noon*. He silently crept along the floor, climbed up onto the back of the couch and dropped onto Cleopatra's head. The ensuing death–roll was terrible. It ended when Spit scratched out Cleopatra's eye. Holding it carefully in his mouth, he returned it to Montrose.

Mia brought the tough but kind girl home for afternoon tea. The two girls tickled Spit's stomach while they waited for their afternoon tea. Mrs Montrose ascertained that Mia's new friend was called Molly and assured Molly she would fit in perfectly with the family. As Mrs Montrose, Max, Mia, Molly and Spit sat by the fire, eating hot buttered scones, they simultaneously sighed with contentment.

Spit started nonchalantly playing with his cat's eye. Nobody took much notice thinking it was one of Max's marbles but then Mrs Montrose took a closer look. "Oh Spit," she said sadly. There was a knock on the door and without even waiting Dr Turner and Kristy marched into the house. Spit decided it was time for some discretion and took himself off to Mia's room. Mrs Montrose quickly put the cat's eye into her cup of tea.

"Cleopatra was worth a lot of money," Dr Turner said. "You can't enter a one–eyed cat in a show, you know. And our polished boards are ruined."

"And we're selling up," Kristy added. "We're moving to Mount Macedon. Much nicer people there. Pilots."

"Pilots?" Mrs Montrose carefully stirred her cup of tea.

"We will miss you, and Olivia too of course, won't we children?"

ALL THAT GLITTERS
by Amy Doak

S o, what brings you to Bendigo?" How original. Inwardly, I cringed. She was definitely one of the most gorgeous women I'd ever seen in my life and I wasn't exactly turning on the charm.

"Such beautiful gold rush history," she said with a heavy accent. "The buildings, they are so pretty. Fascinating stories. I have been travelling from Noosa to Melbourne. I was told Bendigo was an excellent place to stop."

"And how have you liked it so far?"

"Very cosmopolitan," she said. "Wonderful coffee." A smile. I'd made that coffee after all. "But I am sure I'd learn a lot more if a local showed me around."

It would have been rude of me to decline, right? So I offered her a tour once I'd knocked off in the afternoon…if she didn't already have plans, of course.

We got to chatting. She was a traveller, she said. Originally from Poland. Now based in Bali – because it's cheap – and sharing a small villa with about ten others, just like her. A two-room place, "but no one stays there long enough for that to be a problem". I nodded. When I spent that year in London, there were 12 of us in a three room flat in Wimbledon. You make do.

She makes a living taking photos – a beautiful woman in beautiful locations – and then YouTubing and Instagramming and all the other things that go with that.

Later that day, she climbed on the back of my beat up old Vespa with her camera across her body, wearing a completely inappropriate outfit given the time of year, and we went to see the sights.

As the night came to a close, we drove past the lights of the Sacred Heart Cathedral and up to the Poppet Head in Rosalind Park. We climbed to the top and I let her wear my jacket as we looked over the city, lit up as best as a regional city can be on a weekday night in winter.

"Come with me tomorrow?" she murmured, as she wrapped her arms around me and rested her head on my chest.

"Tomorrow?"

"I've been invited," she said. "By your city. To a display. All about the gold rush times and the new gold that is found."

"Oh, yeah. I read about that. They're letting everyone look at The Miner's Thumb. First time it's been showcased in public."

"It is very exciting," she nodded and her eyes gleamed in the moonlight. "After all these years, people are still finding gold here. A funny name, they gave it."

I laughed. "They always seem to give big nuggets weird names. No points for originality on this one though, it does look like some old guy's thumb. Can't believe it was just dug up in a suburban backyard. Wish my dog would do that. The most I get out of him is a chewed up thong."

Being the ultimate gentleman (or a fool? I'm still not sure), I delivered her back to her maisonette with a kiss on the cheek and a promise to return in the morning for the Tourism event. Which I did, with an almond croissant no less.

We walked through Rosalind Park, her hand in

mine, to the exhibition and I couldn't believe my luck.

"I know you're supposed to leave tonight," I said as we walked and ate. "I'd love another day with you though. Maybe after the exhibit we could go to a show at the Capital together? I've got two tickets to a matinee?"

I didn't mention that I bought them that morning while I pulled a sickie from work. Even though I knew someone was bound to see me and dob me in. Bendigo.

"I have to meet with some people..." she hesitated. "But, yes. I will go. That sounds lovely. You are so very sweet."

We climbed the stairs of the Old Post Office and bundled into the Living Arts Space with what felt like the rest of the city. We stripped off coats and I looked across the crowd to where the nugget was sitting safely in its glass cabinet. Richo, one of my mates, was in his security uniform next to the cabinet. We chatted as I watched her work the room with her other 'influencer' friends, taking a stupid number of photos and laughing.

"Can we hold it?" one of them asked Richo with saccharine sweetness.

He smiled back, clearly not as much of a sucker as me. "The mayor and the TV people will be here soon, then everyone will get a go."

I stood back as the main action happened. Amongst the crowd, she stood out, almost glowing as she smiled and chatted with the group. I was realistic enough to know I'd probably never see her after today, but I still couldn't believe my luck.

Her hair, her eyes, her beautiful smile, her elegant hands holding the nugget…hang on. Holding two nuggets. Deftly turning them over and switching out one for the other as she passed it along to the next person.

If I hadn't been watching her so closely, or looking at her hands at that exact moment, I never would have seen it happen. She was that smooth. She dropped the nugget in the side pocket of her bag with absolute ease.

I looked at Richo and the other security guards in the room. Nope, completely oblivious. Looking back at her, she caught my eye and waved me over. I don't know what came over me, but I walked straight up to her, grabbed her tight and gave her the most passionate kiss I could muster.

She reached up and pressed her hand on my cheek, laughing. "I'll be truly sorry to leave you behind."

I kissed her again and then she said, "I must go for photos with the others. I will meet you later, yes? At the Capital."

I knew, with that rock in her possession, that there was no way she was meeting me later, but I wanted to believe her all the same. I nodded, and then she was gone.

Which brings me here. Freezing my bum off on the cold, stone steps of the Capital Theatre. I watch the clouds quickly move in and out of the spaces between the grand 1870s pillars that flank the historic building.

I stand up and look down View Street, stretching my legs, and well, what do you know? Here she comes.

I'd like to believe she came for me. To take a risk. To see a show. To spend more time. To maybe ask me to join her and travel the world. But instead of a kiss, I am greeted with a slap across the cheek.

"Where is it?" she hisses at me, just as two police cars come through the roundabout at the Rifle Brigade, perfectly timed thanks to my call to meet us both outside the theatre.

Who am I kidding, I think as I pull the nugget out of my pocket and hand it over to the cops. Born and bred in Bendigo, why would I ever want to be anywhere else?

THE IMPORTANCE OF KNITTED SQUARES
by Pam Harvey

The dog was the first one in, disappearing head-first, tail an upright flag. Birdy had her eyes on the tail and followed seconds later. She saw the scramble of spotty dog at the bottom of the hole with the lichen-covered rocks at its side, and then a looming dirt lumpiness caught her. Limbs jarred. She grimaced, winded. The little dog licked her face, worry creasing his brow.

"Pepper," she said, the word thick on her tongue.

He wagged his tail and grinned.

Birdy pulled herself into sitting, rubbing her stomach as the pain eased. Above her, the light was round, tunnelled by the walls of the hole. Trees waved casually at her. Already the winter sky was dull. Half an hour, and it would be black.

She stood, ankles rolling on the uneven surface of rocks, branches, bush litter. Pepper sniffed the ground then the damp walls, jumping up to scrabble his front paws against it. Birdy did the same, reaching up as high as she could but the walls had no traction and her fingers slid down. She leaned her back against it, cold seeping through her thin running singlet. "How about this, dog? We're stuck in a mine shaft."

Pepper smiled and sat.

At first she yelled but her voice seemed to fall back down on her instead of projecting forward and no one answered. She felt for her phone but of course she'd left it on her mother's Formica kitchen table among the bunches of sympathy flowers. Then she threw clumps of dirt to land ineffectively somewhere up top. Finally, she sank on her haunches next to her brother's dog, one hand on his warm head, a comfort in the rapidly cooling air.

Evening gathered. The wind stopped but leaves rustled and somewhere up there a kangaroo thumped past. The sky darkened to charcoal. Her stomach ache left and the dog fell asleep on her knee.

In the quiet, Birdy held her Fitbit up to check its tiny screen. "Sixty-one," she said to Pepper, who twitched an ear. Even in the most boring of board meetings listening to self-important colleagues in suits and as fit as she was, she'd only been able to get her heart rate to sixty-five. It was a game she played with slow breathing and a touch of mindfulness – how low could she go? The minute she was out of the room, though, her body fired up to its normal humming self and she met clients bright-eyed and full of zing, heart coursing adrenaline-spiked blood around her body so rapidly she often felt sick.

Sixty-one.

The quiet was heavy but not suffocating. It's like a blanket, Birdy thought. A heaviness of hand-knitted squares sewn together and worn as a throw against the frost. She closed her eyes, listening. A magpie squawked indignantly, fluttered wings, and settled. More kangaroos now, slow loping, tails dragging through leaves. A mopoke sounded, getting in early. There were hundreds of soft sounds in harmony. All it needed was the click-clack of her mother's knitting needles and Birdy would be back where she started, secure and belonging.

The cold in the hole slowly intensified. She pulled the sleeping dog onto her lap and wrapped her arms around both of them. He woke and blinked up at her, the stubby whiskers on his mongrel face tickling her bare arms. Her brother's dog now, but her mother's a few days ago. Jamie had offered him to Birdy but who was he kidding? A dog in an apartment alone for fourteen, sixteen, hours a day?

"It would be good for you," Jamie had said.

"Why would you say that?"

"Because." He'd shifted around the cracked leather armchair uncomfortably.

"What on earth does that mean? I'm out most nights." She sank down into the only other chair in the room, an old rocker with a blanket draped across the holes in its upholstery. "My social diary is as full as my work one."

Jamie had shrugged, clicked his fingers to the dog who pined on his mat, but Pepper curled around himself and lay with his back to them.

"I'll take him for a run."

"It'll be dark soon."

"I know where I'm going."

She did, too, until Pepper veered off to chase a rabbit.

Birdy put her head down to rest lightly on Pepper's body. Jamie was the oldest and he acted like it. He had a partner, three children, and already two dogs. She had no idea how he did it. *It* being life so crowded. At least the people around her disappeared at night as they staggered back to their own apartments and she could take the lift to her little studio existence where the neatly-made bed and the sweep of the kitchen bench was exactly how she'd left it. Exactly.

The dog twitched, chasing rabbits with REM.

Exactly the same and never less than sixty-five.

The hole smelled dank. Moss. Leaves. Maybe the faintest scent of something long dead, nearly rotted away. It was strangely grounding to be reminded that that's how it was in the time capsule of the mine shaft. She wasn't worried that she'd be a permanent part of it. Eventually, Jamie would haul himself away from the photo albums he was packing in boxes and bring his torch to her. She looked up at the sky where the silhouettes of branches were dark against increasing starlight. They were beautiful.

Then some sleeping galahs moved in alarm, indignant from torch beam. They flapped into the branches above them, squabbling in protest. Birdy grinned. The way they complained was, after all, why her mother had called her Birdy. "Come on, Birdy," she'd say. "Time to stir. You sound just like a mob of galahs getting up at sparrow's. Come on, little Bird."

It was impossible to think she'd never hear that voice again.

"Birdy?"

"I'm here!"

Birdy stood up stiffly, tipping Pepper from her lap so he landed on all fours. Jamie's torch light wavered nearer. His footsteps were soft in the damp debris. The light speared down to catch her face. "How did you get down there?"

"Pepper went first."

"Are you hurt?"

"No."

The light disappeared as Jamie went in search of a solid branch then came back as he lowered it down. Birdy tucked Pepper under her arm and scrambled up to hand him over before gripping Jamie's hand and doing an undignified belly-crawl over the edge.

"You're freezing." Jamie wrapped his coat around her.

"I'm fine now."

They started the walk back, Pepper on a tight lead. It wasn't so dark now even with Jamie's torch off. The stars were out in winter glory, their refracting auras like monotoned fireworks.

"Sixty-one," Birdy said.

Jamie tutted. "You've got hypothermia."

"I have not."

"What's sixty-one then?"

"Jamie?"

"What?"

"Can I buy out your share of Mum's house?"

Jamie walked on solidly, nodding like someone who already knew. "You're sure?"

The answer was in the regular pumping of her heart. "Yes."

They rounded the corner of the bush track and there was the low settlement of the house glowing pale with kitchen light. It looked as warm as a hand-knitted blanket.

"Jamie?"

"What, Birdy?"

"I'll have the dog as well."

DYING FOR A COFFEE
by Colin King

Several historic buildings could be dubbed the pride of View Street, but for Detective Sergeant Rory James, that honour always sat with the Wine Bank cafe. The grand former bank—one of six uphill of Charing Cross—served what Rory swore was the best coffee in Bendigo. Its Corinthian columns may have been fewer and a tad shorter than the Capital Theatre's, but the Wine Bank's beckoning aromas led him blinkered past rival splendours. He hunkered on under threatening cloud and fast-ebbing willpower.

Plainly, website writers who insisted Sigrid Dobell's The Manse B&B was within easy walking distance of the View Street cafes had never spent the night going toe-to-toe with Sigrid through a bottle of single malt. Avoiding a pain-steeped morning recovery expedition was as inconceivable as cars making a comeback in Hargreaves Mall. Moreover, he avoided graver impairment by not staying put and ingesting the brake fluid taste-alike that Sigrid passed off as coffee.

Rory stood watching the Wine Bank owner place a 'CLOSED' signboard at the entrance. Rain arrived on cue and song lyrics, near tailored for the moment, spilled from the café sound system.

Standing at Charing Cross in the rain …

His misery was un-ignorable. The owner offered a what-can-you-do shrug.

"Sorry mate. The cops have shut us down. We found dead bodies inside."

Survival kicked in ahead of disbelief. "Is the coffee machine still on?" Rory rasped.

"Nah, and I couldn't make you one if it was. There really are two dead bodies. This place will be crawling with cops."

"Where are these cops then?"

"To tell the truth, that bit really pisses me off. Plumbers found the bodies—and a basement we never knew we had—while they were replacing a burst pipe. Nothing grizzly though … it's like they've been there forever. Borderline archaeological I reckon. The cops ordered a special forensic team from Melbourne, strung up crime scene tape, then bolted. Dunno when they'll show up." He repeated the what-can-you-do gesture. "Bastards. You can tell they've never been in business."

"Turn the coffee machine back on and give me a look."

The owner's bemusement hung.

"I'm a homicide cop. Detective Sergeant Rory James … from Melbourne," he saw fit to add. He showed his ID.

"Am I allowed to do that?" he asked Rory.

"You're not allowed not to, including not turning the coffee machine on. Now, what's your name?"

"Mark Coffey."

Rory hesitated a beat, then decided not to expend pre-coffee words clarifying if that was a barista's real surname.

"Just show me the bodies," he said.

They stared into the unwelcome abyss in the café floor. A massive sheet of slate flagstones, fixed together on the underside, had been lifted at one end and propped with a solid length of timber. Rory pointed to the unlit tradie light dangling at the end of a yellow extension cord — word free communication of the coffee-deprived.

"I'll turn it on," Mark twigged. He found the switch and began showing Rory.

"There's this bloke here, sort of crumpled below where they lifted the slate. His mate's sitting against the back wall. And here's the thing, there's no way in or out. The other cops, sorry police, were totally baffled."

The next track kicked in on the café speakers:

No fortune to be made, Gold filled these shallow graves.

"You want me to turn that off? Penny plays it when she's cleaning up the kitchen."

"Just make sure she's got the coffee machine on."

Rory somehow descended to his knees with the speed—if that's not the wrong word—of a praying mantis on dope.

He scanned the underside of the flagstones for a good while before taking in the scene below. The chalky brick-lined space was too small to be a usable room. It was also too low to stand in without stooping. The figures were skeletal but still draped in their clothes. One had indeed accepted his fate sitting against the back wall. The other body was a contorted heap below the opening. The floor, and some indiscernible debris, was black with damp from the leak. Higher up, the dust laden bodies and walls had morphed to a uniform light-grey.

"The plumbers reckon rats got into them. This bloke has had fingers chewed off one hand."

"Hmm. Did you have any idea this cavity existed?"

"Shit no. I spent a lot of time and money restoring the place myself and I can tell you it's not on the old plans. And I don't think the National Trust knew about it. They bought and owned the building for a long while after the ANZ branch closed in the nineteen-seventies. It's probably a basement remnant from the original chambers they knocked down to create this classic in the eighteen-seventies."

Money goes out quicker than it comes in ... That's our cash grab.

Rory noticed the band had added horns and Hammond organ on this track, evoking the might of Bruce Springsteen's E Street Band.

"Who's the band ..." he asked Penny as she came past with a bag of rubbish, "...and have you got that coffee machine going?"

"It's the Four Lions. Their 'Vahland' album, I think. Fiercely-local musos if you hadn't guessed ... and yeah, the machine's warming up."

Rory gave an unsmiling thumb-up and turned back to Mark.

"Anything else you can tell me about when the

place was being built?"

"Not really. You won't find much in the archives either because the builder shot through a day or two before the bank moved in. It must have been one of those jobs that sends a builder broke. These slate flagstones for instance were literally worth their weight in gold. The whole lot was brought from England as ship's ballast. When it was offloaded in Port Melbourne, they restored the ship's balance for the return journey with vaultfuls of Bendigo gold."

Rory unfolded his body from its kneeling position even more slowly than he'd gone down. He continued studying the subterranean scene as he thought aloud.

"I reckon Penny's *Four Lions* nailed it. This was an attempted cash grab. These blokes went in there intending to emerge a couple of nights after the bank moved in and help themselves. And it has to be your missing builder. No one else would have access to the space, or know it even existed. Trouble was, one of them got his hand caught under the slate as they lowered it. It would have been too heavy for the other bloke to lift it off on his own ... they died trapped in a soundproof tomb. The body of this poor bugger eventually fell away from his fingers. They're still up here."

He pointed.

Mark bent under the propped sheet of slate. The white insides of four finger bones were adhered to its underside lip. They had split apart like pea shells when the slate was lifted. No doubt the other half of the finger bones remained fixed to the ledge where the slate had rested for nigh on a century and a half — somewhere under the plumber's mud-caked boot prints.

Mark straightened, clearly impressed. Rory spoke first.

"Now, how about a double-shot long black?"

DISCLAIMER AND ACKNOWLEDGEMENTS:
The historic crime portrayed in this story, and its perpetrators, are entirely fictitious. The Wine Bank was actually built by the much-respected George Pallett who also built Bendigo's town hall and railway station. Pallett Street in Golden Square is named after him. The Wine Bank architects, Alfred Smith and Arthur Johnson, also designed Melbourne's Supreme Court and St Kilda's famous music venue, the Esplanade "Espy" Hotel. Thank you to Bendigo's fab Four Lions for permission to use their song lyrics. Thank you too to Wine Bank owner, Mark Coffey, for allowing himself to be portrayed fictionally.

LEAP OF FAITH
by Lauren Mitchell

I count the dead bodies on my drive to work. Every day there are at least two new ones, freshly bloating by the roadside. Death and decay is now part of the daily commute yet its normality is shocking. I'm dreaming of them. Jumping out from behind trees, jumping over the car, skidding under it, playing chicken, bounding in great mobs over barbed wire, kicking up dust.

They have a death wish, these kangaroos. Ron at the butcher's shop gives me news of their whereabouts. "There's usually a mob just before the Sebastian turnoff," he said yesterday, "next to that paddock of old machinery. We call it Hopper's

Crossing." I know the spot. It's been ten weeks since we moved from the city of Bendigo to the tiny town of Raywood and I'm learning to tick off the landmarks along the 28ks between home and town. Lone donkey in a paddock, tick. Stone cottage with dormer windows, tick. Turn off to the Woodvale Public Hall, tick. And now, Hopper's Crossing.

"It's only 15-minutes' drive from the Star Cinema!" I say to anyone who baulks at the name 'Raywood'.

"Oh, how civilised," says a friend. "I thought you'd moved to the Wild West."

I don't mention the strange, eight-pronged tumble weeds gathering by the back door.

We couldn't believe our luck when our offer was accepted on the house. Hulking goldfields-era heritage, polished and painted white. Not a straight surface in the place, yet four mature trees in the backyard. Four! (No one can afford a decent backyard in Bendigo anymore.) And just a pub and a butcher's shop for neighbours.

"How'ya settling in?" Ron asks, over crumbed schnitzel and the *Herald Sun*.

I knew this was our house when I saw the ad in the paper. You know how you wait for a sign? You wait and wait and resign yourself to the fact that everything is random and we're just clumps of stardust, earth bound and tumbling around and around. But that's just it. We are energy, and I felt it that day when I turned the newspaper page and saw the ad. I felt a sign. It came in an almighty surge and I literally sat bolt upright, like a Looney Tunes character. It was nuts. It sent us on a rollercoaster of events and emotions and we braced ourselves until finally landing in this place. (A neat way to gloss over two months of buying, selling, packing a home of 15 years, moving and signing endless icky legal documents.)

I read somewhere that moving house changes you. Learning how to live in a new environment, among new people and places changes the sense you have of yourself. Slowly, slowly, I get that. This tiny town has thrown me out of the comfort of old routines. We're learning the rhythms here. The drinking habits of pub dwellers. The school bus timetable. The rising and setting of the sun. The sky is so big and the landscape so flat that I feel the days, arching. And I feel the dusk-to-dawn encroachment of kangaroos. "They won't be so bad when it rains," assures Ron. I hope he's right.

I've taken to Classic FM in the mornings. It infuriates the teen in the front seat, but placates the tot in the back. His tiny feet kick to the great symphonies. Cello concertos in B-minor, Vivaldi's famous *Four Seasons* and the odd work of opera. Oh, we're not that cultured, but it does calm and focus me for the drive. For 28 kilometres the world slows and the senses sharpen to detect grey bodies, dead and alive. It's like being in a film, at the beginning of the crucial third act when the main character elopes, all is lost and frantic strings accompany a car careering down a lonely stretch and you're braced for yet more disaster and bang!

When I was a child my older brother insisted we pull over for every dead kangaroo. He was a serial pouch-checker, disappointed to return to the backseat empty handed. Just once he found a joey, while he was off riding his bike. Our mother tumbled it into an old pillowcase and hung it over a kitchen chair and we watched the weight of it there. Saw the shapes of legs through thin cotton. The next day it went to a wildlife carer.

I know what it is to carry a child just so, as every mother does. The burden of that body, growing heavier and heavier, arms and legs jabbing organs. The responsibility of it. This second child of ours came of his own accord. There we were, heading towards a secure sense of our future selves, when bang! Pregnant, after six years of hoping and six of giving up. We'd have a baby and a teenager. That's not a thing. You don't see families like that in new car commercials. 'Just. Keep. Breathing,' I'd tell myself, when nauseous beyond belief, bedridden and barely hanging on to sound mind and body.

Should I be checking these bodies? What sort of person am I, who would drive past a mother, freshly hit, while my own child burbles and coos to Bach in the back? I wonder what it would be like to find the opening and slip my hand inside a kangaroo's pouch. Would it feel like the mink coats in that vintage store in View Street, turned inside out? Would it stay warm in there for long?

Evenings here are getting cooler. We're inside earlier. We're on the couch, watching cooking shows. Justine Schofield is on a boat, barbecuing kangaroo. On a boat! The significance is hard to see. She only just sears the fillet because, she says, it's so lean if it's not prepared rare it's too tough. She whips up a side of steamed asparagus, cuts medallions of bright red meat and arranges it just so on a big white plate. It looks barely dead, and I'm reminded that meat is flesh and flesh is what we're all made of, and again there are very few degrees separating me from the grey ladies lumped by the bitumen.

I know another mum who lives out here. We make small talk about the dangers of driving home after dark. "I'm slowing down to 60 at night," she says, "I'm counting at least two new kangaroos each morning."

"Me too!"

"I had to pull one off the road last week."

What? Yes. On the way into town she pulled out and around the car that had hit it, plus others who'd stopped to help. On the way back home the body was still there, half on, half off the road, wholly dangerous. "Luckily someone stopped to help me," she said, "because it was much heavier than it looked. At least 50 kilos." That's about my weight.

This morning there is a crescendo in the fifth symphony when I see her, intact yet certainly dead. She wasn't there yesterday. I feel a surge of something strong and I recognise it. It's a sign. I pull over as far as I can. I park between spindly grey box. I tell my sons I'm getting out to check for a joey. The teen looks up from his mobile phone. The baby burbles something incoherent. I slowly crunch through dry grass. I crouch beside a blank black eye. My heart is thumping in great bounds. I find the pouch. It welcomes my hand and I'm shocked it feels of clammy skin. I find a slender leg, a dense tail, a heartbeat. Yes. "Just. Keep. Breathing," I say, and I'm talking to both of us.

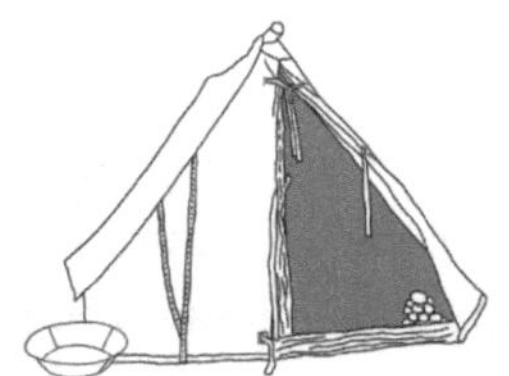

PROFITABLE ENVY
by katrina Nannestad

When Tom and Molly Wilson drove onto the goldfields at Eaglehawk, jiggling and swaying atop their loaded wagon, eyes boggled and tongues stood still. Not that there was anything odd about another wagon, another couple setting up camp, another fool of a husband hoping to strike it rich among the wattle and rocks of central Victoria.

The eyes were boggling at Molly. She smiled and nodded at everyone she passed, like a queen deigning to notice her subjects. She wore feathers in her bonnet, lace across her bosom and a brooch the size of a chook's egg at her throat. Furthermore she was clean - not a speck of dust nor a smear of clay about her.

'What a sight!' snorted Mrs Wotherspoon when the wagon passed and her tongue was set free. 'A few days here and she'll lose her shine!' She lifted her washing from the tub. Muddy water ran from pants that used to be white.

Mrs McInnis, who was next in line to use the tub, smirked. "A few days? As soon as she leaves the top of that chariot her skirt'll be hemmed with dirt. And by the time she's cooked their mutton for dinner, there'll be flies galore tangled up in those feathers. I give her three hours and she'll be bawling her eyes out, begging His Lordship to take her back to the city."

A little lad ran past, his dusty buttocks bare for all to see.

"Billy!" shouted Mrs Wotherspoon. "Get back into the tent until your duds are dry!" She rolled her eyes at Mrs McInnis and sighed, "Look how this place drags us down. We all become savages in the end."

But Molly Wilson would not be dragged down. She would not be dragged to the brink of despair. She would not even allow the hems of her skirt to be dragged through the dirt. She remained clean and perky, flitting gaily across the goldfields, calling upon a tent a day like a fine young lady visiting the best homes in Toorak.

In Mrs Wotherspoon's tent, a small jug sat on a

crate that served as dressing table, larder or dining table, depending on the time of the day. "Oh how charming!" cooed Molly, sitting the jug on the palm of her hand. "My mama has an entire dinner set in the same pattern!"

In Mrs McInnis' tent, a clock sat in pride of place on a three-legged table. Molly ran her slender white fingers across its face. "My papa has a clock like this," she said. "It sits on the bench in his stables. They're funny little things aren't they? Never keep time. Inside, of course, Papa has a grandfather clock… mahogany… accurate… glorious!"

In Mrs Kelly's tent, Molly seized upon a straw bonnet. "Good gracious!" cried Molly. "I remember when these were in fashion! So quaint to see one still being worn. My sister, Nora, is married to a bishop and has a new bonnet made for every season."

And so Molly strutted from tent to tent, poking, prying and prattling, leaving fury, envy and discontent in her wake.

When Molly next made her social rounds, the women of the goldfields were better prepared. Best feet were forward. Some were even shod with freshly dusted boots!

Mrs Wotherspoon offered Molly a piece of damper and treacle. The plate was chipped but the knife was a hefty silver affair, tarnished, but of good quality.

"Seven more where that one came from," whispered Mrs Wotherspoon.

"England?" asked Molly, eyes wide and innocent.

"No!" Mrs Wotherspoon cackled. "The bottom of the mattress, stuffed into the straw!"

Mrs McInnis plonked her baby boy into Molly's lap the minute she arrived. The boy was gumming on a heavy gold chain from which dangled a fob watch, also gold. "I forgot all about that old thing," Mrs McInnis smirked, but her blushing cheeks gave away the lie. "Got to the bottom of the tea caddy and there it was!" She glanced at a sack of flour sitting in the corner and lowered her voice. "It's not the only treasure tucked away in here, mind you."

Mrs Kelly happened to be wearing her Sunday best when Molly visited, even though it was Wednesday. Her Sunday best was the same filthy dress she wore every other day, with the addition of a brooch. "It was my grandmother's," bragged Mrs Kelly, thrusting her ample bosom forth so that Molly could better see. It was exquisite, a perfect pearl set into a fine gold leaf.

Molly smiled. "Your brooch is very… delicate."

Mrs Kelly detected a criticism in the word. "I have a bigger one!" she snapped, and she drew a brooch as big as Molly's fist from beneath her pillow. It was made of a dozen chunks of coloured glass and sparkled like the shards of a broken rum bottle in the midday sun.

"Oh how lovely," gushed Molly. "Now that is what I call a brooch!"

And so Molly skipped from tent to tent, watching, listening and learning, making murmurs of surprise, nods of approval and blushes of envy so crimson that even the most obtuse women were flattered.

The womenfolk felt rather smug. Molly Wilson might not have been dragged down to their depths, but they had shown that they could most certainly rise up to meet her heights!

It seemed fitting, then, when the note arrived – written on real stationery – inviting them all to tea at the Wilson camp, further along the creek.

"There'll be a china teapot," said Mrs Wotherspoon. "Royal Doulton. Not a billy in cooee of the table."

"Linen serviettes," hissed Mrs McInnis.

"Real chairs to sit on," gasped Mrs Kelly.

"Shortbread."

"Ham sandwiches."

"Fresh milk!"

"A fancy tea!"

"We'll have to mind our p's and q's."

On the blessed day, the women bathed and primped. The cheek of every child was polished with spit and the corner of an apron. Then, as one, the women and their young-uns headed along the creek bed.

But at the end of the long walk, the Wilson campsite was not to be found. No tent. No Molly Wilson. No china teapot. Not even a crumb of shortbread.

"Perhaps they've moved camp!" cried Mrs Wotherspoon squinting between the ironbark trees. "Further up the hill. Closer to Mr Wilson's mine."

An old timer approached with his nag. "Mr Wilson 'as no mine," he growled.

"Of course he does!" snapped Mrs McInnis.

"I know what I see." The old fellow chuckled. "While your menfolk are blastin' and diggin', crushin' and sievin', Mr Wilson is loungin' in the shade, readin' books, sleepin'."

"Lounging? Reading? Sleeping?" gasped Mrs McInnis. "But how do the Wilsons expect to make their fortune?"

Baffled and irritated, the women herded their children all the way back home. But home was in disarray - beds upturned, pillows slashed, rugs crumpled, holes dug in earthen floors, tins tossed and everything covered in a dusting of flour.

Slowly, painfully, the truth dawned upon them. One by one, they ran from their tents, faces red and sweaty, mouths wide and bawling.

"My silver knives are gone!"

"Harry's nuggets have been filched!"

"My money tin's dug up!"

"Walter's fob watch is missing… and the silver rattle… and granny's pearls!"

"We've been diddled!"

Only Mrs Kelly remained calm. She swaggered from her tent, fingering the ugly coloured-glass bauble at her throat. Her treasure was safe. She alone had outwitted Molly Wilson!

Mrs Kelly stared at her pathetic neighbours. She smirked and nodded with satisfaction.

And so did Molly Wilson as she jiggled and swayed atop the loaded wagon, a sack of treasure tucked beneath her toes, a gold and pearl brooch of dazzling value pinned to her throat, and a happy restful husband at her side.

THE KNOWING STONE
by Steve Proposch

Today:

I'll pretend I'm writing an email on my phone purely to appear normal to the Hungry Jack's. Once I'm done and rested I'll leave. I'll stand and tuck the phone away in my pocket with a quiet, satisfied smile as if I've just done something clever, and no one will be impressed.

Crowded through a trashy city with no space to rest alone. I think of quiet. I long for country.

Tomorrow:

I think of a word for work every work day. Usually it's bogus, boring, bitter, exhausting, emotionally exhausting (sometimes it's two words), grinding, or too looooong. Occasionally it's brilliant (sarcastically). Bearable, okay, not-too-shabby and interesting appear frequently on a rising scale. Then there is the extremely rare exhilarating (in its literal sense). I am thankful for those days. Satisfying is an equally infrequent choice and runs a close second place in regard to being thankful about it, and, thankfully, it is the perfect word for today. I've put in the effort. I've engaged with the platform; I've questioned and answered; I've handled objections with an icepick; I've sold ice-bucket loads of a semi-decent product that nobody needs from a widely known historical brand name you can trust. I pitched that waste like it was well-cut diamonds. I was liked. I was appreciated. I managed. I was calm and measured in my responses. I got things right. I got my name on the board. It was a satisfying day (big sigh). Back to this bullshit tomorrow.

Yesterday:

If I'm still writing on my phone when I come down it will seem perfectly fine. Right now it feels obvious and super-normative, like I'm acting out and not really writing. But I am really writing, right? I tell myself it's not the people I've been before it's me, now, and it's now now, you know? No? What I mean is it's not then, you know? Many yesterdays ago I was a bloody menace to society. I can see that now but couldn't get vision on it then. Anger was just something that happened and beneath it all I believed I was still a really nice guy so it was all good, but that kind of behaviour is really unacceptable; smashing plates and slamming doors just because something wasn't going my way. Punching walls. Storming out of the house because I'd run clean of arguments but still felt this bubbling, burning mood spiking through me and I couldn't calm down without some kind of action. Boiling blood. Who invented that phrase? It feels like you're boiling when you're angry for sure. Screeching tyres down the driveway and burning up the street like a stupid idiot. Entitled, adolescent, an easy out of any situation. Later on you come back and say you're sorry and that it was about something else, not you, and you'll never do it again. But I always did it again. And what if I'd ever hit someone while driving in that mood? It scares me now, that thought. It embarrassed me then if ever I took time to witness my own actions (rare) but the feeling's worse now because I'm older and can see more angles on it and it's terrifying to think about stuff I did then that was careless and dangerous and the lives I could have destroyed including my own and my family's. You have to be so thankful for all the disasters that don't befall you in life I reckon.

People don't realise that. A lot of people only think about the stuff that has happened and are thankful (or the opposite) for that, but if they really looked back and thought about all the sad and nasty things that haven't occurred then I reckon they'd be a hundred times more thankful than they already are. And if stuff has happened to them that is sad and nasty it may not seem quite so debilitating in the bigger picture of all the fantastically bad and sad and nasty things that could have happened too. I dunno. Depends I suppose. Ironically it's the sad and nasty things that have helped me to realise this is true.

Here Comes Another One:

Smoking in an alley now but I swear this woman thought I was stalking her just before. It was only that she was walking too fast for me to pass and too slow for dropping back. I was reading the crowd, navigating between islands, doing my best not to bump into anything or anyone. There wasn't a gap to be had for two blocks. I sped up to try to get past at one point and she sped up too, turning her head just a fraction my way so I knew she knew I was there. It felt creepy, as if I was being creepy but all I was doing was walking the same way. Another time there was a woman sitting alone on the station at Southern Cross on one of those long seats that have two sides so you can sit either side, and I walked past her towards another seat down the line, but I walked behind her, not in front, because the seat I wanted was in that direction, and she nearly startled when I went past. Again that fractious glance, like she's checking my position in relation to her, thinking about the pepper spray, keys and/or nail file in her backpack and how she could get to them fast if she needs to. She would totally take me down, no regrets. I'm hopeless in a fight. She was steeling her resolve as I passed by and not letting me out of her sideways sight as I got to my seat. I felt yucky. I wasn't doing anything out of my way and I got that bad vibe from a person who knows nothing about me. Which is totally fair enough when you think of everything women have suffered at the hands of men. I wish those days were over, but I'm not so innocent as I feel. That anger I had. Broken furniture, slammed doors and screeching tyres. That violence was me. It is me. I wish I wasn't like that but … My smoke has gone out. The woman has walked on. Back to this bullshit.

Wasted:

The bloody Swanill has done it again. This time there's only three carriages and two out of three are reserved seating so it's standing room only in the stalls. I've managed a seat but there's a dad and two boys squished up with me in the grubby four-seat pod and they're going all the way to Mildura and their reserved space was double-booked so they should really be sitting in the reserved carriage instead of bumping up against me and every stinking human stepping on toes in this crappy old train. Maybe they should get a new tag line – V/Line: Carrying the Stink of Humanity Since 19... whatever! Nice though (the dad and two boys, not the Swanill).

Sometimes I read on the journey home. People seem so awesome when you read about them. Seeing or watching things about people can get pretty deep too, even when it's shallow, but something about reading goes all Jules Verne on that. Certainly it's better than when you actually talk to people about themselves. That can be really boring.

They say that when you write you have to look hard at who you are and come from there. Writing is too personal to fake. People can spot a fake a mile away. Some people are professional fakes and it's like everyone knows but nobody says anything. That's not for me. I'm not a nationalist and I'm not a rationalist. I'm not religious and I'm not extremist. I'm not political or very cynical. I can say a lot of things I'm not, but can't pinpoint exactly what I am. Suburban? Yes, soooo endlessly suburban. Soft?

No doubt. Stupid? Absolutely. That's not me being humble. It's inherently true that I'm piss-poor at politics, mathematics, metaphysics, mechanics, any kind of science, and languages. What did I miss? Art. The only thing I'm good at is feeling. I felt my way through all those wasted years of brimming life, sexy and hungry and smart and cosmopolitan; knowing everything by knowing nothing. I could get away with that once. I chanced it. We built a cult around it: The Knowing Stone. And we were so stoned when we thought about it and we laughed at every rule we made up. It was debauched from the beginning, we decided. Any old cult can descend into debauchery. We wanted one that just kicked off that way. We built an idol from slate and sandstone near an old mine shaft in Barkers Creek and took off our clothes and danced around it, off our heads. It was a squat-bodied structure with a head of stones arranged so as to leave a gaping hole, like an eye. As a final touch we set a small shard from a broken mirror in the hole, and that evening as the sun was setting it unexpectedly bounced off that mirror and for a brief shining moment we knew we were special in this world.

Sent from my iPhone

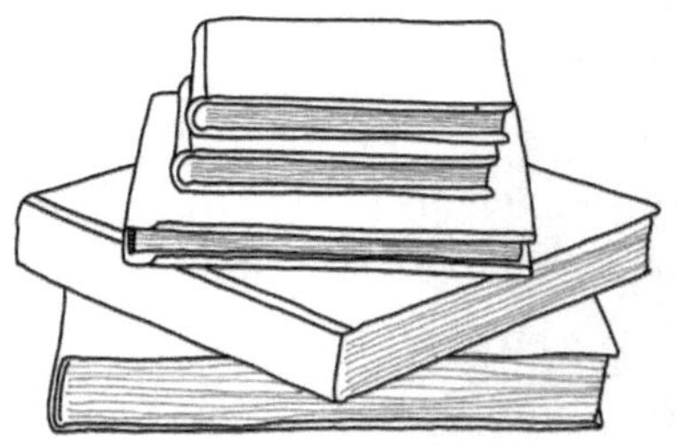

AUTHOR PROFILES

S ally Abbott is a former journalist and PR consultant who lives in Castlemaine in Central Victoria. She was the inaugural winner of the Richell Prize for Emerging Writers in 2015 and her first novel, *Closing Down*, was published by Hachette Australia in 2017. She is currently working on her second novel.

Jess Anastasi has been making up stories ever since she can remember. Though her messy handwriting made it hard for anyone else to read them, she wasn't deterred and now she gets to make up stories for a living. With a multi-award-winning science fiction romance series to her name, her books feature larger than life heroes with relatable vulnerabilities who find themselves in situations that push their resolve to the limit. Jess is a tea-addict who loves loud music, dancing in her kitchen and a good book on a rainy day. A fangirl at heart, she probably spends too much time watching too many TV shows.

92

Carmel Bird is a novelist and short story writer who lives in Castlemaine. She was the winner of the Patrick White Literary Award in 2016. Her manuals for writers, *Writing the Story of Your Life*, and *Dear Writer Revisited*, are widely used, and she is a popular leader of workshops for writers.

Her next novel, *Field of Poppies*, will be published in November 2019.

John Charalambous was born in Melbourne and moved to Bendigo in 2007. His first novel, *Furies*, was published 2004, and was shortlisted for the Commonwealth Writer's Prize Best First Book. His second book, *Silent Parts*, was longlisted for the Miles Franklin award in 2007, and later adapted by screenplay writer Blake Ayshford into the telemovie *An Accidental Soldier* (2013).

John's most recent novel, *Two Greeks*, whilst not a memoir, draws on elements of his parents' marriage and life growing up in a culturally mixed family.

Dianne Dempsey is a novelist, book reviewer, screenwriter and journalist. While she has written for the *Age*, the *Sydney Morning Herald* and the *Australian*, Dianne says most people get excited when she says she used to write for *Neighbours*.

She currently works at the *Bendigo Weekly* part time and is researching a non fiction book on the impact on families of returned war veterans.

Amy Doak is a writer and independent publisher. In 2005 she launched *Bendigo Magazine* and in 2009 she launched *Little One Magazine*, which sold in 16 countries.

Amy is the author of four books and has worked as a co-author on many others. Her publishing company, *Of The World Books*, and its imprints, *Fiosracht Press* and *Accidental Publishing*, have published over 14 titles in the last three years.

Pam Harvey lives in Mandurang South and has never accidentally spent time down a mine shaft. She has published short stories, children's fiction, and women's fiction, and regularly reviews books for ReadingTimeOnline. Her writing grants include a VicArts Creators grant and a May Gibbs Creative Fellowship. She writes in the cracks between working at her day job and being with her family.

Colin King is a Bendigo writer, who grew up in Horsham and worked as a major-projects consultant for the Victorian state government before retiring to write. Along the way, he has played guitar in rock bands, ran marathons, led trekking parties and hand built a weekender on the Grampians fringe.

His debut novel, *A Vintage Death*, was first published in 2013. Its launch was a special event at that year's Bendigo Writers Festival. His second novel, *Wetland*, was published in 2018.

Lauren Mitchell has been telling Bendigo stories for almost 20 years. She has written for local and national newspapers and magazines and is the author of five books, including the popular *Artist Spaces* series.

Lauren hosts regular author talks at the Eaglehawk Library and writing workshops from her historic goldfields home. Apart from words, she loves winter picnics, midday moons, mugs of tea and her (slightly unconventional) family.

Katrina Nannestad is a children's author. She grew up in country NSW in a neighbourhood stuffed full of happy children. Her adult years have been spent raising boys, teaching, perfecting her recipe for chocolate-chip bickies and pursuing her love of stories. Katrina celebrates family, friendship and belonging in her writing. She also loves writing stories that make children laugh.

Katrina now lives on the side of a hill in central Victoria with her family, a mob of kangaroos and an exuberant black whippet called Olive. Her books include *The Girl, the Dog and the Writer* series, the *Lottie Perkins* series, the *Olive of Groves* series, *When Mischief Came to Town* and the *Red Dirt Diaries* series.

Steve Proposch is publisher and editor of *Trouble* magazine. Previously he has edited the seminal street press magazine *Large* and has had fiction, poetry and non-fiction published in various magazines and literary journals. Recently, together with co-editors Bryce Steven and Christopher Sequeira, he has edited the three volume *Cthulhu Deep Down Under* anthology series and *Cthulhu Land of the Long White Cloud* (IFWG), as well as *War of the Worlds Battleground Australia* (Clan Destine Press), with more projects in the works including an exciting new anthology featuring high profile internationally recognised authors due for release in 2020.

Goldfields

Tania Ryan is the founder of Petit Pixel Design, where she specialises in digital storytelling via illustration, animation and video. Tania has worked with corporate clients, authors and indie businesses for projects that have been published both online and in hardcopy.

A Bendigo local, Tania creates in her home studio (with her dog working as assistant!) and can often be found drawing with a coffee and a podcast in local cafes.